E V $ 15.88   ATA
Vainio, Pirkko.
The Christmas angel

PRESS
CARD
HERE

Other books by Pirkko Vainio
available from North-South:

Don't Be Sacred, Scarecrow!
The Snow Goose

Copyright © 1995 by Nord-Süd Verlag AG, Gossau Zürich, Switzerland
First published in Switzerland under the title *Der Weihnachtsengel*
English translation copyright © 1995 by North-South Books Inc.

First published in the United States, Great Britain, Canada,
Australia, and New Zealand in 1995 by North-South Books,
an imprint of Nord-Süd Verlag AG, Gossau Zürich, Switzerland.

Distributed in the United States by North-South Books Inc., New York.

Library of Congress Cataloging-in-Publication Data is available.
A CIP catalogue record for this book is available from The British Library.
ISBN 1-55858-499-4 (TRADE BINDING)
1 3 5 7 9 TB 10 8 6 4 2
ISBN 1-55858-500-1 (LIBRARY BINDING)
1 3 5 7 9 LB 10 8 6 4 2
Printed in Belgium

The Christmas Angel

WRITTEN AND ILLUSTRATED BY

Pirkko Vainio

TRANSLATED BY ANTHEA BELL

North-South Books

NEW YORK / LONDON

It was beginning to get dark, but shining Christmas lights brightened the streets of the town. Maria waited outside while her mother was shopping. She wanted to look at all the little lights. They turned into stars when she squinted her eyes.

She noticed across the street a window filled with toys, and went over to look.

Maria gazed in delight at all the toys. Suddenly a face appeared in the window glass. It was the reflection of a bearded man. Maria turned around.

An old man in a ragged coat was standing behind her. Scared, Maria ran.

"Where have you been, Maria?" asked her mother crossly. "You were supposed to wait for me here. You might have been lost in the crowd!"

Maria was out of breath. "I saw something!"

"I know, I know, you saw all the toys you'd like to have. Come along now."

"But I saw—"

"We must hurry home, Maria. Grandma's expecting us."

Tonight Maria and her grandmother were going to bake special Christmas cookies. What Maria liked best was icing and decorating them.

They baked hearts, stars, moons, and angels—so many that there was hardly any room left on the kitchen table for their supper.

After supper Grandma said, "Why don't we bring down the Christmas tree decorations now?"

They climbed the stairs to the attic. Inside a big old trunk, underneath the glass baubles and the star for the tree, Maria found a little package wrapped in tissue paper. It was an old music box with the figure of a little girl on top.

"I was given that when I was your age," said Grandma.

"She's so pretty," said Maria. "She looks like the angel in the window at church. But of course she doesn't have any wings!"

Grandma smiled. "I've heard it said that real angels are born without wings. They have to earn them by doing a good deed."

"But how can a china angel do a good deed?" Maria asked, studying the music box.

"Maybe someone has to do it for her," suggested Grandma as she brushed the dust off the little figure's dress and carefully put the music box back in the trunk.

Early the next morning, while Maria's mother was still sleeping, Maria and Grandma went to church together. Maria stopped in front of the stained-glass window. Rays of sunlight lit the window and made the angel's wings glow. Maria could just imagine it flying. She stood for a long time, staring at the angel.

They walked home through the park, and Maria saw the old man there, sitting on the grass in the snow.

Maria squeezed Grandma's hand. "I saw that man before, in town," she whispered.

"Poor old man," said Grandma, sighing. "To think of him sitting out here in this cold weather!"

"Doesn't he have any home?"

"I don't think so."

"But he's feeding the birds. Where did he get the bread?"

"I expect he searches for things to eat."

"You mean he has to search for food?" asked Maria, horrified. "Even at Christmas?"

Grandma nodded, and before they turned the corner, Maria turned to look back at the old man once again.

Maria's mother was in the kitchen when they got home. She had found a big glass jar for the cookies Maria and Grandma had baked the night before. "I've put them in this so we won't be tempted to eat them," she said. "Otherwise we'll have nothing left but crumbs on Christmas Day."

"I saw an old man in the park feeding pigeons," said Maria. "He has nothing but crumbs to eat too."

"I know," said her mother, and that was all. Grandma didn't seem to know what to say either.

Maria began cutting out paper stars. Now and then she glanced out of the window at the snow, and wondered if the old man was still sitting in the park.

Maria couldn't get to sleep. She had so much to think about. She thought of the toy-shop window with all those lovely toys. But the old man came into her mind as well. Then she thought of Grandma's music box with the wingless angel perched on it, and she remembered the big angel in church.

All of a sudden the room seemed to be filled with warm light. Maria didn't know if she was awake or dreaming.

The next morning Maria got up early. Very quietly she went downstairs to the kitchen, and very quietly she pushed a stool over to the counter, climbed up, and lifted down the jar. She took out all the cookies shaped like angels and put them in a paper bag. She fastened the bag with some of her paper stars and put it in her coat pocket.

Then Maria switched on the light and bustled about setting the table for breakfast, being sure to make a lot of noise.

Soon her mother came into the kitchen. "Well, you're up early!" she said. "I suppose you were too excited to sleep because it's Christmas Eve!"

"Yes . . . well . . . no. I want to go and feed the pigeons."

"Very well," said her mother, and she gave Maria some old crusts of bread.

The snowy streets were still empty as Maria hurried along. When she neared the park she saw the old man sitting on a stack of old newspapers. Quietly, she went closer, brought out the bag, and quickly put it on the man's lap.

When the old man looked up, Maria had already run away.

In the afternoon Maria helped to decorate the Christmas tree. Her mother had threaded string through the cookies so that they could hang from the tree. The crescent moons, the stars, and hearts looked very pretty.

"I thought we had some angels, too," said Maria's mother in surprise.

Maria didn't know where to look.

Her mother stared at her intently. "Oh well," she said finally, "I suppose they've flown away."

Maria blushed. Then she confessed what she had done.

Later that evening they lit the candles on the tree and sang carols. Grandma read a story, and then Maria was allowed to open her presents. The last package of all contained the music box with the little angel on the lid. As Maria lifted it from the tissue paper, she stared in wonder.

"Oh, Grandma!" she cried. "Look! It has wings!"

Grandma studied the angel carefully. "How extraordinary!" she said, shaking her head. Then she smiled at Maria. "I expect someone did a good deed for her."

Maria, her mother, and her grandmother all sat and admired the angel.

"Don't you want to hear the music?" asked Grandma after a while. So Maria wound up the music box. They listened as it played a Christmas carol, and watched as the angel began to turn and turn, her wings aglow in the candlelight.